GRANDPA'S INHERITANCE

"AN UNEXPECTED LEGACY THAT CHANGED EVERYTHING"

SHALOOM NIYOMUVUNYI

To my lovely mother,
whose unwavering love, quiet sacrifices, and endless
prayers built the foundation of everything I am—
this book is a reflection of your strength and grace.

To my dear brother,
my first friend and lifelong companion—thank you for
walking beside me through every season of life,
for the laughter, the late-night talks, and the unspoken
understanding.

This story, Grandpa's Inheritance: An Unexpected Legacy
That Changed Everything,
is for you both.
Your love has been the greatest legacy of all.

Shaloom Niyomuvunyi

Contents

Contents

Contents

FOREWORD

In every culture, there exists a figure who speaks with timeless truth, whose words echo beyond their years. For me, that person was called grandfather. He didn't speak loudly, but his words lingered. He didn't offer solutions, but he offered strength. This book is a collection of those moments—those porch conversations, silent glances, and steady hands that guided me through storms.

Each chapter is a tribute to the kind of wisdom we often overlook in our pursuit of the extraordinary. What you'll find here is ordinary truth, beautifully lived.

This is not just Grandpa's inheritance to me—
It is now, humbly, my gift to you.

Preface

I did not write this book to impress the world.
I wrote it to remember... and to honor.

This began as a private archive of thoughts—memories that came to me during quiet walks, late-night reflections, and those rare moments when a scent or sound would bring back Grandpa's voice like a gentle wind.
I was never told to write them down. But I felt it—deeply—that they were not mine to keep alone.

These lessons were not taught in a classroom. They were lived. They were whispered across dinner tables, spoken under stars, or left unsaid but deeply understood. Some were carried in silence for years before they ever made it to the page.

Grandpa's Inheritance is not about money or land. It is about the invisible wealth that shapes a life: wisdom, kindness, patience, dignity, and love that doesn't boast but never breaks.
This is the kind of inheritance that does not get spent, but shared.

If this book reaches your hands, I believe it's because you, too, carry someone's story in your soul.
And if a single page helps you heal, hope, or hold on a little longer—then Grandpa's legacy has lived on through you.

Thank you for being here.
— Shaloom Niyomuvunyi

Acknowledgements

This book carries many hearts within it—some still near, some remembered with love.

To my Unseen Grandpa, whose words became my compass, whose silences taught me more than noise ever could, and whose life was the first story I ever truly loved—thank you for being my quiet hero. This book is yours before it is mine.

To my beloved mother, the heartbeat behind every sacrifice and the light behind every hope—you are the first place I ever felt safe. Your prayers and tenderness gave me the courage to dream and the strength to write.

To my brother, my lifelong friend, and the constant reminder that love doesn't need to be loud to be real thank you for standing beside me when I had nothing to offer but faith.

To every reader, who opens this book with an open heart—thank you for listening to my story and for allowing Grandpa's wisdom to speak softly into your world. If you find comfort, clarity, or courage in these pages, then this journey has been worth every word.

To all those whose names may never be printed but whose love shaped me anyway—thank you. Your kindness lives quietly in these pages.

With a heart full of gratitude,
Shaloom Niyomuvunyi

Prologue

The Porch Where Time Stood Still

They say wisdom comes with age, but not all wisdom is written in books or spoken in grand halls. Sometimes, it's whispered between sips of tea on a weathered porch. It lingers in the pauses between stories and glows in the soft light of sunset reflecting off an old man's eyes. That's where I found it—on a creaky swing, beside my grandfather, wrapped in silence and stories.

This book isn't about fairy-tale legacies or fortunes measured in gold. It's about the kind of inheritance that can't be taxed or stored in a vault—the kind that lives in our hearts and guides our hands. It's about hard truths told with a soft voice, and quiet lessons carved into memory.

What my grandfather gave me wasn't loud. It didn't come in the form of lectures or commands. It came as a slow unfolding—of reflections born from heartbreak, insights gleaned through loss, and joy found in the simplicity of a well-lived life. His words were gentle, but they carried the weight of generations. His stories, seemingly casual, were roadmaps to integrity, love, and purpose.

This is his gift to me. And now, through these pages, it's my gift to you.

Take a seat beside us. The evening is young, and Grandpa has a few more things to say.

Epigraph

"Sometimes the most powerful sermons come from the quietest voices."
— Anonymous

I

STRENGTH IN LOVE AND RESILIENCE

My old father told me one day, "Even if your parents were imperfect, love and honor them. You wouldn't be breathing today without them."

He sat down and said with calm determination, "When life pushes you to the edge, don't break—bend. This is the time to be strong."

He once looked me in the eye and said, "If others speak poorly of you, don't lose sleep. Let your goodness be your defense."

He said with a sigh, "Some people will dislike you simply because your light reminds them of their darkness. That's not your burden."

I remember him saying, "Steer clear of those who are obsessed with their own importance. They take offense when others shine."

He leaned in and whispered, "Never let wealth turn you into a stranger to your own values. Money can be earned again—trust cannot."

He reminded me during hard times, "When your pockets are empty, your true friends will still come around. Watch for those few."

He said plainly, "Be kind, but don't mistake kindness for obligation. Not everyone has your heart."

He taught me, "Financial success means little without character. Be known for how you treat others, not just what you own."

And when I asked him about friendship, he said, "I don't care if a friend is rich or poor—as long as they are loyal and speak no evil of me, that's enough."

One day, leaning back with eyes closed, he said, "No one builds a good life by lying. A lie might bring comfort, but truth always catches up."

He asked me seriously, "If you could choose again, would you still choose your spouse? If the answer is no, reflect on why."

He warned, "Don't let onlookers distract you. They're often the loudest critics and the least helpful."

He told me, "Don't marry someone who makes you bitter toward your family. Marry someone who inspires you to be better."

Then, smiling, he added, "Treat me well, and I'll treat you even better. It's that simple."

He leaned forward with a tired breath, "Budgeting becomes exhausting when there's too little to budget."

Then, with a grin, "People with flat noses are often the most beautiful—maybe nature knew they'd be goddesses with any more blessings."

Growing serious again, he said, "Those who speak bluntly and boldly often have the purest hearts."

He shared, "Irony lives in how the ones who wronged you play victim to your silence."

His voice dropped, "Apologies are easy; rebuilding trust is not. I forgive, but I don't forget."

He said dryly, "You say I have a bad attitude. Maybe I do. Why should I be the only one kind when you won't be?"

Then he laughed, "If I'm the devil in your story, I guess you must be the fallen angel."

As he aged, he told me, "You stop craving noise. You begin to value peace over proving a point."

He said, "We may be broke, but we know how to be grateful—and that makes us rich."

He looked out and remarked, "Degrees don't guarantee respect. I've met educated people with no manners."

He added, "Often, those who laugh the most are hiding the deepest pain."

He warned me again, "No matter how hard you hustle, you'll never outrun the consequences of deception."

Then, half-joking, "Stop acting like a saint on Facebook. Your profile may go to heaven, but you won't."

And with a smirk, "If a post doesn't name you, don't claim the guilt. Sometimes silence keeps your dignity."

Finally, he said, "Even if you stay home every day, your neighbors will still have stories to tell. Let them talk."

II
LIFE'S IRONIES AND QUIET WISDOM

One evening, as the sky glowed in fading amber, my old father sat beside me on the porch swing, his steps slower, but his thoughts sharp as ever. The sun dipped low behind the trees, and he began speaking as if he were emptying his heart one truth at a time.

"Life," he said, "has a way of giving its best lessons through silence and strange timing."

He took a slow sip of tea and began his litany of wisdom—each sentence simple, but heavy with truth:

"Stay humble when success finds you. That's when pride sneaks in wearing your own smile."

"There's no shame in being poor—but pretending to be rich when you're not? That's where dignity crumbles."

"Trust is like breath on glass—clear when fresh, but gone in a moment. Guard it, and don't waste it."

"When people hurt you, don't respond in anger. Just remember how easily they broke what was once whole."

"Kindness doesn't need wealth behind it. A soft word to a bitter soul can shift an entire day."

"Irony lives in how the loudest boast of peace but start the quietest wars behind your back."

"Let your work speak. If it's good, people will know. If it's not, no amount of shouting will change that."

"Forgiveness is freedom. But don't confuse being forgiving with being foolish."

"I once helped someone who later mocked me. That's the irony: those you lift up may someday try to step on you."

"Some people will only respect you when you're no longer available to be stepped on."

"Your grandmother used to say: 'If you must borrow respect, it's not real respect.'"

"People often envy what they don't understand. They will mock what they secretly desire."

"Be cautious of those who flatter too quickly. Often, their loyalty ends the moment yours is tested."

"There will be times you do everything right and still lose. That's not failure—it's redirection."

"Silence isn't weakness. Sometimes, it's the loudest message you can send."

"The people who forget your kindness first are often the ones you sacrificed the most for."

"You'll find that the ones who talk most about loyalty often struggle the most to live it."

"Not everyone clapping for you wants to see you win. Some just want to be close when you fall."

He looked out at the hills, the light now almost gone, and said quietly:

"Don't be bitter when life is unfair. It's not always about you. Sometimes it's just life being life."

He paused and added one last piece, his voice softer than the wind:

"Real wisdom doesn't come from being right—it comes from being quiet enough to understand when it matters."

III

A FATHER'S LEGACY: SUCCESS, DIGNITY, AND UNSPOKEN TRUTHS

As the stars blinked awake in the darkening sky, my father leaned forward, his voice softer, yet clearer than ever. He didn't raise it, but somehow, each word struck deeper than the last.

"Success," he began, "isn't how much you earn—it's how much of yourself you don't lose while earning it."

"I've watched people spend their whole lives chasing money, only to realize their children just wanted time, not toys."

"My greatest pride was never the money I made—it was seeing you and your siblings grow, finish school, and find your way."

He looked out toward the horizon. "You don't owe anyone an explanation for being misunderstood. Let your life speak. It speaks louder than defense ever could."

He continued, his voice steady, "In hard times, remember those who stayed. When things get better, let your loyalty speak louder than your success."

"Repay kindness, even years later. Never forget who fed you when your hands were empty."

"I've met men with degrees who lacked basic compassion—and others with little education but hearts full of wisdom. Intelligence without kindness is just noise."

"Faith isn't what you wear to church; it's how you treat the janitor, the stranger, the ones who can't repay you."

"When life collapses—jobs, homes, money—hold tight to your integrity. If you have that, you still have something God can bless."

"Miracles don't always knock. Sometimes, they arrive while you're sleeping, disguised as tomorrow."

He paused, his voice slower now.

"Some of the people you'd die for won't even flinch for you. Learn this, but don't harden. Not everyone can love the way you do."

"Your value doesn't disappear just because someone fails to see it. Their blindness doesn't cancel your worth."

"Three things to avoid at all costs," he said firmly:
"Luxury that puts you in debt."
"Pride that isolates you."
"And jealousy that turns love into resentment."

"Stay grounded. Work with clean hands and a quiet heart. Dignity isn't loud, but it sleeps well."

He turned toward me, and I saw the tears he didn't try to hide.

"These aren't just things I've learned," he said. "They're the bruises and blessings of a full life. I give them to you so you don't have to earn them the hard way."

IV

LESSONS OF LOVE, RESPECT, AND LIFE'S BEAUTIFUL STRUGGLE

As the night deepened and the stars blinked awake, my father's voice softened. He spoke not with authority, but with warmth—the kind of warmth that only comes from someone who's lived through hard days and still chooses love.

"Your mother," he said, adjusting his cardigan, "showed me what real love looks like. It's not flowers or chocolates—it's going without so her children never had to."

"She prayed every night—not for herself, but for you. For your safety, your future, your happiness. That's what mothers do. Their prayers are silent armor."

He paused, wiping a tear he didn't try to hide.

"Whatever you become in life—and I know you'll achieve plenty—never forget to honor your mother and me. Not because we're flawless, but because we gave you roots before you earned wings."

"Respect isn't blind obedience. It's recognizing the sacrifices that made your freedom possible."

"People will judge you without knowing you. Don't chase their approval. Just remember, even in darkness, God sends help from places you'd never expect."

"I've met men with prestigious degrees and empty souls—and farmers with nothing but wisdom in their words. Education is useless without humility."

"If someone from your past comes knocking again, pause. Ask yourself why they left. Not all returning faces come with good intentions. Be kind—but stay smart."

He smiled gently. "Your mother never wanted luxury—just enough to provide for you. Her joy was in your joy. That kind of contentment? That's wealth."

"People today gather friends like trophies. But in storms, trophies don't shelter you. Better to have a few friends who hold your hand than hundreds who only 'like' your posts."

"When your heart breaks—and it will—cry if you must. But then stand back up. That's what makes struggle beautiful: it shapes strength."

"Success isn't proving others wrong. It's proving yourself right. That you didn't give up when life dared you to."

"As I've grown older, I've learned to let go. Anger is poison you drink, hoping others get sick. Let it go. Choose peace every time."

He looked me in the eye and said, "Some people will lean on you endlessly, then vanish when you need them. Keep helping—but remember to leave some kindness for yourself."

"If I could ask God for just one thing," he said quietly, "it wouldn't be riches. It would be strength for our family to handle whatever comes—with grace, not fear."

"Success," he said, "isn't measured by square footage or brand names. It's looking in the mirror and being proud of who's looking back."

"The world might not always see your light—but don't dim it. Don't become what's common: nosy, bitter, or cruel. Stay gentle. Stay you."

Then he chuckled and added, "And when people frown at you for no reason, maybe it's not you. Maybe they're just low on vitamins."

The porch fell quiet again, but his words stayed with me like stars that linger long after sunrise. Years later, as I pass his wisdom to my own children, I finally understand: the lessons weren't meant to be followed—they were meant to be lived.

V
MY GRANDFATHER'S EVENING WISDOM

The evening breeze grew cooler as Grandpa tucked his blanket around his legs. He rocked gently in his old chair, the rhythm as steady as his voice when he spoke truths that only age can teach.

"You know," he said with a smile in his eyes, "getting older doesn't just bring aches—it brings clarity. What once felt confusing becomes obvious, like morning fog lifting to reveal the road beneath it."

He gazed up at the stars and began offering the kind of advice that doesn't come from books, but from surviving what life throws at you:

"Set boundaries—not to shut people out, but to remind them what's sacred. Dignity doesn't shout; it simply stands firm."

"Don't raise your voice to draw the line. Let your self-respect be the fence that quietly says, 'This is mine—you don't cross it.'"

"After the factory shut down and life got quiet, I found out who truly cared. The friends who checked in during my silence—those are the ones worth keeping."

"Your grandmother used to say, 'A medal on your chest means less than kindness in your heart.' I still believe that. Character matters more than any award."

"Some people turn themselves into victims of their own stories—stories they wrote and keep retelling. Don't get pulled into their fiction. It's spiritual quicksand."

"Never confuse gentleness with weakness. Life may hit hard, but staying soft inside is a quiet kind of courage."

"Keep your circle small. Not everyone belongs at your table—even if they want a seat, not everyone earns one."

"Dream big, but don't panic if the path changes. If one plan breaks, make another. What matters is that you keep moving forward."

"The hardest truth you'll face as you grow? You can't make anyone choose you—not friends, not family, not love. Sometimes, paths run parallel without ever meeting."

He paused then, his eyes following a firefly drifting through the dusk.

"You know what makes me proudest?" he said after a while. "Seeing you take even the smallest risks to build something new. That's how life gets better—one brave step at a time."

He leaned back, his voice softer now.

"The ones who stand with you while you're still in pieces—those are your real family. Doesn't matter if they're blood or not."

The jasmine-scented air carried his words across the porch, and I sat there quietly, letting them sink in.

Those moments weren't just conversations—they were the inheritance he gave me. Quiet wisdom passed through fire, not just words, but a way of seeing the world.

And now, years later, as I sit with my own children beneath similar stars, I share these same truths, adding to them the lessons I've gathered. That's how wisdom lives on—hand to hand, heart to heart.

VI

NAVIGATING LIFE'S CHALLENGES WITH WISDOM AND GRACE

The night was still, and Grandpa's voice took on that slow, thoughtful rhythm that always meant something important was coming.

"You know," he began, adjusting his glasses, "I've learned to trust what people do more than what they say. Words are like wind—easy to scatter. Actions? They leave roots."

He sipped his cold tea and continued:

"Don't mistake endless patience for kindness. I once waited too long on people who never meant well. The kindest thing I ever did for myself was to finally walk away."

"And strange as it sounds, walking away didn't hurt—it healed."

"Never announce your victories too soon. Let them ripen in silence. The moment you speak too loudly, the frost of envy may come."

"People who dislike you for no reason are often the ones paying closest attention. Let them watch—that's their obsession, not your problem."

"Sometimes, God removes people from your life for a reason you'll never hear. It's mercy in disguise. Don't chase after what was divinely cut off."

"Promise yourself peace of mind. Build it like a home and defend it like a fortress. Don't let opinions, mistakes, or fear live in your head rent-free."

"The sweetest success is doing exactly what others said you couldn't. Not to prove them wrong—but to prove to yourself that they never defined your limits."

He smiled gently, the memory of my grandmother clearly in his mind.

"She used to say, 'A diploma may hang on the wall, but real education walks beside you in how you live.'"

"True education is in how you treat a waiter, how you handle conflict, and how you respond when no one's watching."

He leaned forward slightly, eyes glowing in the porch light.

"Be a goal-chaser, not a fault-finder. Some folks spend all their time criticizing from the sidelines instead of running their own race."

"Stay close to those who talk about the future. Distance yourself from those who constantly resurrect the past."

"And if you weren't invited, don't show up just to feel included. Late invitations and half-hearted gestures are messages—read them, then move on."

"Your value was never tied to someone else's seating chart."

His voice dropped to a near whisper.

"When people can't control you anymore, they'll try to control how others see you. Don't stoop to explain yourself to small minds."

"Stand tall in who you are. The ones who matter won't need an explanation. The ones who need one, don't matter."

The crickets sang softly as the wind stirred the porch swing. Then came his final, most piercing truth:

"The greatest test of loyalty? It isn't who stays during the good times. It's who protects your name when you're not around to defend it."

VII

LESSONS FROM GRANDFATHER ON SUCCESS AND PEACE

The night had settled in quiet harmony. Only the wind whispered through the trees as Grandfather sat in his old chair, hands folded, eyes lost in memory.

"You know," he said gently, "when I was young, I thought success meant applause. Recognition. A title. I thought it wore a suit and answered to 'sir.'"

He smiled faintly and adjusted his flannel shirt.

"But real success," he continued, "is when you no longer need the world's approval to feel valuable. It's when your soul finally stops begging for what was never meant to fill it."

"Peace," he said, "doesn't come from finishing something. It comes from knowing you're enough—even if the world says otherwise."

"Sometimes, the wisest thing you'll ever do is walk away from noise disguised as love."

"The fewer people in your life who stir chaos, the more clearly you'll hear your own thoughts."

He shifted in his seat, the porch swing groaning softly beneath him.

"Experience will teach you what no book can. But be warned—her lessons come with a cost. And she'll keep repeating them until you get it."

"Wisdom isn't measured by how much you've heard—it's measured by how much you've lived through and grown from."

He looked up at the sky as the first stars flickered to life.

"Being a good person won't guarantee others see your value. Don't let that shake you. Some people can only recognize worth when it comes with a price tag."

"Never trade your peace of mind to explain yourself to someone committed to misunderstanding you."

"The toughest lesson?" he asked, his voice softening. "Forgiveness. Not the kind that rebuilds a broken bridge—but the kind that lets you stop standing on its ruins."

"Some connections are better left as memories. You can forgive without reopening the door."

The air turned cooler, leaves rustling like distant applause.

"Let go of what disturbs your calm," he said. "Even if it once felt important. Peace isn't passive—it's a choice you must keep making."

Years later, I still hear those words in quiet moments—like echoes across time. Each one, a lantern. A compass. A reminder that success without peace is hollow, and peace without self-respect is incomplete.

VIII

EMBRACING SOLITUDE: GRANDFATHER'S MIDNIGHT MUSINGS ON PEACE AND WISDOM"

The hour grew late, and the moon climbed higher, casting silver light across the porch. Grandfather's voice softened to a near whisper, not from weariness, but from the weight of what he was about to say.

"You know," he began, eyes fixed on the sky, "being alone isn't the same as being lonely. There's a peace in solitude, like sitting in a quiet garden where your thoughts can bloom without interruption."

He smiled gently and leaned back.

"When I was younger, I apologized for everything—as if my presence needed permission. But peace came when I stopped shrinking myself for the comfort of others."

"That said," he added with a knowing glance, "when you're truly wrong, say sorry with your whole chest. A real apology is rare, and it's priceless when done right."

The scent of jasmine floated in the air as he continued:

"One thing life will teach you—watch who disappears during your struggle. If they couldn't sit with your silence, they don't deserve a seat at your celebration."

He paused, then leaned forward slightly.

"A man chasing a dream needs more than applause—he needs belief. Find someone who doesn't try to rewrite your vision into their version. That kind of support is gold."

The porch swing groaned softly as he rocked back and forth.

"Don't waste breath arguing with those who have no interest in understanding you. Some people speak just to respond—not to hear. Walk away without bitterness. That's power."

His eyes flicked toward the stars.

"You won't be for everyone—and you shouldn't be. If you're constantly adjusting who you are to fit, you'll lose yourself in the process."

He pointed up at the sky, following the trail of a falling star.

"When a season ends, leave with grace. Don't force what no longer fits. Not every ending is a failure—some are exits for your protection."

Then he said, quieter still:

"Be careful not to confuse consistency with growth. Staying the same isn't strength—it might be fear. Be brave enough to evolve, even if it means outgrowing people you once loved."

He shifted again in his chair.

"If someone wrongs you and says sorry but keeps doing the same thing—that's not an apology. That's performance. Don't clap for it."

The midnight breeze passed softly between them as if carrying each truth to memory.

"These aren't just lessons," he said at last, "they're coordinates for the soul—quiet directions I had to chart through years of mistakes and milestones."

Now, as I sit with my own children under different stars, I pass these truths on—new layers added to the wisdom he left behind. His voice still echoes in the still moments, reminding me that living well isn't about being perfect. It's about being honest, brave, and kind, especially when it's hardest to be.

Each generation finds its own constellations, but it's the old stars—the timeless truths—that keep us heading home.

IX

BEYOND BEAUTY: THE TRUTH OF CHARACTER AND INNER STRENGTH

My old father sat beside me, his eyes carrying the heaviness of things learned the hard way. There was no bitterness in him—only clarity. He exhaled slowly and spoke like someone passing down truths that life carved into him over time.

"Believe me," he said, "the day always comes when those who mistreated you wonder why you stopped answering. And by then, you'll have outgrown the need for their apology."

He looked ahead, into nothing and everything at once.

"When I look back, I see mistakes, loss, pain. But when I look in the mirror, I see a man who stood up after each fall. That's what matters."

His voice hardened slightly.

"If you're waiting for a narcissist to admit the truth, don't hold your breath. Their stories always make them the victim—or the hero. Never the cause of the damage."

He chuckled, shaking his head.

"Some people think ignoring me is punishment. I consider it peace and quiet."

Then his tone turned serious.

"I don't care how beautiful someone is—if their spirit is toxic, their beauty is just decoration over rot."

He leaned in closer.

"Behind every strong person is a battle no one saw. A moment when they had to choose—sink, or fight their way to shore."

He let silence stretch before continuing.

"I found peace the day I realized some people were never fighting me—they were fighting themselves and using me as the mirror."

He looked down for a moment, then said:

"Sometimes life hurts not because you're a bad person, but because you kept giving to those who only knew how to take."

Then came a quiet smile.

"Be careful not to waste your life wishing for things you don't have. What you have now was once all you hoped for."

His voice softened as the night deepened.

"You need very little to live a joyful life—once you understand what life is really about, the rest becomes noise."

He tapped his chest gently.

"Funny how your spirit senses something's wrong before your eyes ever catch up. Don't ignore that feeling."

Then with calm certainty:

"Worry won't change what's coming. It only steals the strength you need to face it."

His eyes glinted with truth.

"In life, you get to choose your pain. Discipline hurts now. Regret hurts forever. Choose wisely."

He looked at me and said plainly:

"I used to carry people who wouldn't even stand beside me. That's how I learned not all loyalty is mutual."

And finally, he gave one last piece of advice:

"Never be ashamed of how you earn your living. Work is work. And pride won't put food on your table when you're hungry."

Those weren't just statements—truths sharpened by time and softened by love. I carry them now, not just in memory, but in how I walk, how I speak, how I rise. And as I pass them to my own children, I know this isn't just advice—it's legacy.

X

SINKING OR SWIMMING: THE STORIES BEHIND STRENGTH

The mentor sat calmly, his voice steady—firm, but not harsh. Every word landed with the precision of someone who had learned life's lessons the hard way, one wave at a time.

"Haters," he said, "only hate what they wish they could have—and the people they wish they could be."

He glanced sideways, his expression sharp.

"That quiet feeling in your gut? Don't ignore it. That's not fear. That's your intuition trying to protect you before the damage shows up."

Then he smiled thoughtfully.

"If it ever comes down to being right or being kind, pick kindness. It wins in ways pride never will."

He leaned back, more serious now.

"If someone wants to talk to you, they will. If they want to stay, they will. Don't force loyalty where there's only convenience."

He laughed lightly to himself.

"The plan is simple: move smarter, not louder. Outgrow, outlast, outlove—without explaining a thing."

Then came a truth wrapped in calm reassurance.

"Everything feels hard at first. So if it feels hard, that just means you're in the beginning. Keep going."

His voice dropped slightly.

"I can handle bad choices. What I can't handle is dishonesty. If you mess up, say it. Don't hide behind lies."

With a slight shrug, he added:

"Worrying is like paying rent on a problem that may never even show up. Save your energy for real battles."

His eyes narrowed just a bit, not with anger, but understanding.

"You can't control what others do. Loyalty has to come from within—it can't be bought, begged, or forced."

He paused, looked straight at me.

"When you finally stop caring what people think, you'll feel freedom most people never get to taste. It's fierce. And it's real."

Then, half-smiling:

"Sometimes, I let them lie. I sit back and listen—because it tells me everything they think I don't know."

His expression turned serious.

"You're weak if you let someone talk you out of loving someone who's always had your back. Disloyalty rarely starts loud—it starts with a whisper."

He shook his head, almost amused.

"It's funny how people blame you for their storms—until you step away and they're still standing in the same mess."

Then came the truth no one likes to hear.

"If you want to be great at anything, you better get used to being questioned, judged, and underestimated."

And with a final warning, he said:

"Stay away from anyone who refuses to admit their faults—but never misses a chance to highlight yours. That kind of blindness isn't ignorance—it's arrogance."

These weren't just reflections—they were survival notes. Each lesson carried the salt of struggle and the shine of clarity. Whether you sink or swim, the decision often starts in the mind. And those who learn to float through judgment and rise after betrayal? They don't just survive—they lead.

XI

FINDING PEACE AMIDST THE CHAOS: A FATHER'S INSIGHT

The wooden swing creaked gently beneath us as evening wrapped the sky in gold. My grandfather's voice, weathered and warm, flowed like the breeze—unhurried, but full of weight.

"You know, child," he said, rocking slowly, "dreams aren't just wishes. They're work. If you want them to live, you have to get up and breathe life into them."

He smiled softly before continuing.

"The older I get, the less I care about being understood. You'll waste your peace trying to explain yourself to people committed to misunderstanding you."

He pointed toward the horizon.

"Build things no one can take—your character, your mindset, your honesty. Everything else fades or can be taken. But who you are? That's yours forever."

I asked him, "But what do you do when people hurt you?"

He paused, his eyes gentle but firm.

"Stay kind. Stay soft. But don't let the wounds rewrite who you are. That's how bitterness wins."

He looked at me with quiet seriousness.

"There's a big difference between enjoying your youth and gambling with your future. Fun should never come at the cost of your foundation."

He ran his hand along the porch rail, nodding thoughtfully.

"Words mean less than action. Talk is cheap and easy. Pay attention to what people do—that's where truth hides."

He chuckled, not bitterly, but with clarity.

"The moment you stop trying to impress people, your real life begins. That's when you start showing up for you."

His voice dipped into something softer—gratitude, maybe.

"Pain shaped me. Struggles built me. I wouldn't trade the hard days—they made me someone worth being proud of."

Then he patted my hand and looked into my eyes.

"Don't wait for others to bring joy to your doorstep. Plant your own flowers. Paint your own skies. Decorate your soul like no one else ever will."

Those evenings weren't just conversations. They were quiet awakenings—truth spoken not to impress, but to guide. And now, I carry those words like a compass, finding peace in the middle of life's storms by remembering where my roots are, and who I am becoming.

XII

MORE LESSONS FROM GRANDPA'S PORCH

The crickets had begun their nightly song, and the porch felt like a place suspended between time and memory. Grandpa rocked slowly in his chair, his words soft, but every one of them landed with purpose.

"Patience," he said, "isn't just waiting. It's trusting that the storm will end, even while you're still standing in the rain."

He smiled, almost amused with himself.

"I've always been blunt. Some people call it a flaw—I call it honesty in its most undiluted form. You don't have to be cruel to be truthful, but you shouldn't lie just to be liked either."

He looked at me steadily.

"Keep a few things sacred: your biggest dreams, your deepest feelings, and your personal wins. Let your life speak for you—louder than your voice ever could."

The porch swing creaked as he adjusted his weight, staring off into the night.

"Life threw punches at me, but I never laid down. I didn't survive because I was lucky—I survived because I chose not to quit."

His voice softened as he leaned forward.

"If you've ever loved deeply and it didn't work out, don't feel ashamed. That kind of love says more about your courage than it does about the outcome."

He tapped his cane lightly on the floor, more to emphasize than to fidget.

"Be careful who you let build on your foundation. Some people will take everything you offer, and when the structure's solid, they'll finish it with someone else. Don't be bitter—but don't forget."

His eyes were full of reflection, not regret.

"Strength isn't always loud. Sometimes it's in your ability to let go without anger. It's choosing peace over proving a point."

He gave a faint smile.

"You don't need to fix every false story told about you. Time is good at sorting truth from noise."

As the stars blinked into view above the treetops, he sat back in silence, letting the moment settle.

Those nights on the porch weren't just about passing the time. They were about passing the torch. Every word he offered felt like a seed—quietly planted, waiting to bloom as I walked further into life.

XIII

A GRANDFATHER'S REFLECTIONS ON LIFE AND CHARACTER

The wind carried a quiet chill through the trees, and the porch was blanketed in golden light. My grandfather rocked slowly, watching the world settle into autumn's stillness.

"You know," he began, "the hardest time to stay consistent is when no one's watching—no praise, no reward. That's when you have to be your own applause."

He smiled slightly.

"Truth isn't always gentle. Sometimes it stings before it soothes. Don't avoid it just to keep someone comfortable—truth has its own way of healing, even if it arrives wrapped in discomfort."

He raised his cup slightly, as if in an invisible toast.

"There are three kinds of people worth remembering—those who loved you when you were low, those who left when you needed them, and those who challenged you to grow. Each one shaped you."

The wind moved through the porch rails, and his gaze wandered as he continued.

"If something is meant for you, it'll happen in its time. You can't pull open a rosebud and expect beauty—it blooms when it's ready."

He took a quiet breath, his voice thoughtful.

"Pain doesn't just hurt—it teaches. It slows you down so you notice more. Some call it overthinking. I call it earned wisdom."

The porch swing creaked as he shifted.

"Loyalty is beautiful. But don't confuse it with blindness. Be loyal, yes—but never to the point where you betray yourself."

He looked at me with steady eyes.

"Failure isn't the enemy. It's the guide. You'll trip, fall, get bruised—but each scrape is a lesson in disguise."

Then he said, almost in a whisper:

"There are people who will lift you in prayer, and others who will tear you down behind a smile. The strongest souls are often tested the hardest. And those are the ones who rise."

The last light of the day flickered through the trees.

"Let life unfold. Forcing outcomes only brings frustration. Sometimes the best thing you can do is let go of control and trust the process."

And then, his voice dropped into something deeper—meant to stay with me.

"When people get a dose of their own behavior, they often don't like the taste. But don't concern yourself with that. Let karma do the talking. Your job is to walk forward—quietly, fully, and free."

He leaned back as the sky deepened into twilight.

"Wear what life gave you, not with shame—but with pride. If your experiences fit you like Cinderella's slipper, don't apologize for them. They've made you who you are."

His words didn't come with thunder or fire. They came like falling leaves—gentle, inevitable, and lasting. Years later, I still carry them like a compass tucked inside my heart. And now, I speak them forward, just as he once did from the porch that taught me more than any classroom ever could.

XIV

WINTER WISDOM

Winter blanketed the world in quiet, the kind of silence that invites reflection. The fireplace crackled gently, casting golden light across the room as Grandpa and I sat together, wrapped in warmth and wisdom.

"You know," he began, stirring his tea with slow intention, "the loudest critics usually have the least understanding. They judge your path without knowing what it took for you to keep walking."

He leaned back, eyes steady with remembrance.

"This year taught me something hard: you can't keep pouring yourself into people who don't fill you back. It's like watering soil that refuses to grow anything in return."

The fire snapped softly as he continued.

"Trust," he said, "is a gift wrapped in vulnerability. When you give it, you're offering someone the ability to hold or harm you. That's why you choose who holds it very carefully."

He placed his hand on his chest.

"That voice in here? Your intuition? It doesn't need proof or permission. It knows. If you learn to listen, you'll save yourself a lot of trouble."

He shifted in his chair, the fabric rustling like old pages turning.

"I've made peace with this—when you feel something deeply, either say it clearly or don't say it at all. Half-truths do more harm than silence."

Outside, snow fell slowly, softly—like time itself was pausing.

"Pay attention to what people do, not what they say. Words are easy to dress up, but behavior is where the truth lives."

He looked into the flames, voice low and certain.

"Some people will claim they've been wronged while never admitting the hurt they caused. It's okay to create distance from those who rewrite the past to protect their ego."

Then, after a pause, he said something that stayed with me long after the fire dimmed.

"Growth doesn't always feel like winning. Sometimes it feels like waking up to truths you didn't want to see."

The snow danced outside, weightless and quiet.

"And regret," he added, "rarely comes from mistakes—it comes from the chances we were too afraid to take. Don't wait too long to try."

Those nights by the fire weren't just moments—they were lessons dressed in warmth, handed down with patience. Grandpa's words weren't meant to be perfect. They were meant to be true. And in their quiet truth, I found direction.

XV

SPRING'S NEW BEGINNINGS

As blossoms unfolded and the morning light kissed the earth, Grandpa and I sat quietly in his garden, surrounded by color and calm. He tended to the soil like it was something sacred, each movement deliberate and full of care.

"You know," he said, watering a small sprout with steady hands, "I didn't learn generosity because I had extra. I learned it because I once had nothing, and I knew how that felt. That kind of emptiness teaches you how to give."

He looked toward the rising sun.

"Every day deserves a fresh beginning. Start it with something good—a thought, a prayer, a quiet moment. Positivity first, and the rest of the day will follow your lead."

As butterflies drifted lazily across the garden, he leaned on his shovel and continued.

"Distance doesn't always mean rejection. Sometimes it's the best way to protect your peace—like these garden fences. Boundaries don't keep people out, they keep your joy in."

He knelt beside a row of blooming flowers and smiled.

"See these plants? None of them need anything from each other to bloom. That's the secret—grow beside others, not for them. Live with appreciation, not expectation."

Standing slowly, he brushed dirt from his hands.

"People will judge you no matter how carefully you live. So live freely, truthfully. And stay away from tables where gossip is served. If you won't feed that fire, you'll never get burned."

His voice held a quiet power now.

"Sometimes moving on feels like losing—but later, you'll see it was pruning. Letting go hurts in the moment, but it clears space for something better."

He looked around the garden, proud of its colors and calm.

"Don't cling to what's fallen. Be thankful for what's still blooming. And stay hopeful—because every season holds something beautiful."

Then, placing his hand gently on my shoulder, he said:

"I'm building a life that feels good because I finally believe I deserve it. And you do too, little one. Don't ever settle for anything less."

Those spring mornings became more than just garden visits—they became sacred lessons in how to grow, release, and bloom. Grandpa didn't just teach me how to care for the earth—he taught me how to care for my soul.

XVI

THE LAST SUMMER EVENING

The sun hung low, casting warm light across the porch where we sat for one of our final talks. Grandpa's voice was slower that night—softer, but filled with clarity. There was something sacred in the way he spoke, like he was wrapping each word in the care of goodbye.

"You know," he began, his eyes watching the horizon, "I spent a lot of years putting everyone else first and leaving myself last. I used to think that was noble—now I know that taking care of yourself isn't selfish. It's survival."

The golden light faded, and he paused.

"To anyone carrying sadness in silence, I'll say this—healing takes time, but it will come. Maybe not today. Maybe not next week. But one day, you'll feel light again."

He leaned back into his chair, his hands resting in his lap.

"Some of life's worst pain has a strange way of building something beautiful. Like how fire can make a forest grow stronger—your hardest seasons often lead to your strongest self."

A soft breeze moved through the porch as he continued.

"Don't spend your nights thinking about those who never think of you. And never tie your happiness to money. Joy has always been free—you just have to look in the right places."

He took a slow breath, inhaling the scent of the warm summer air.

"When things feel heavy, remember—tomorrow could change everything. Keep working. Keep hoping. The right people, the right moments—they'll arrive when they're meant to."

Then, with a small smile, he added:

"Sometimes life needs a reset. That's not failure—it's just realigning. Don't carry other people's bitterness on your back. Their attitude isn't your assignment."

The first stars began to appear, faint and steady.

"When you're hurting, remind yourself—it won't last forever. Pain is like weather. It moves through, but it doesn't stay."

He turned to me then, his eyes filled with quiet strength.

"There's something powerful in being alone—not lonely, just with yourself. That's where you remember who you are, and why you matter."

And finally, as the sky turned deep blue and the world fell quiet, he gave his parting truth:

"Life's doors are always open—for entering, for leaving, for starting again. Just make sure you walk through each one with purpose, with peace, and with your head held high."

That last summer evening didn't end with a grand speech or dramatic farewell. It ended the way all his wisdom did—gently, firmly, and full of truth. His words became part of me. A compass I'll carry, even now that he's gone.

Through every storm, every sunrise, I return to that porch in my heart—and I remember.

XVII
SACRED TEACHINGS

As summer gave way to the stillness of autumn, Grandpa and I found ourselves wrapped in misty mornings and deeper conversations. These were no longer casual reflections—these were his sacred teachings, spoken with the tenderness of someone who had learned every word the hard way.

"Life," he said, sipping his coffee slowly, "isn't always gentle—but it's honest. What you survive becomes your teacher. What breaks you becomes your blueprint."

He looked toward the garden, where dew clung to every leaf like a memory.

"Go where you're valued, not just seen. A small room filled with understanding is worth more than a stadium full of strangers clapping for the version of you they don't even know."

His eyes twinkled with quiet humor.

"Sometimes I wish life came with background music—so we could sense the mood before it shifts. But silence," he said, "is often the clearest sound. Listen closely when everything else is still. That's when you'll hear what matters."

As leaves began to fall around us, he continued.

"God's plan rarely looks like our own. It's not always smooth, but it's always purposeful. The moments you feel forgotten? That's when the roots are growing deeper."

He sat back, the weight of memory resting in his voice.

"I've learned more from the difficult people than the kind ones. They showed me exactly who I never want to become—and for that, I'm oddly grateful."

Then, with a knowing smirk:

"Funny thing about those who don't like you—they pay the most attention. Let them. Give them a front-row seat to your growth."

His voice shifted into something quieter, more certain.

"When people lie to tear someone down, it always circles back. Not instantly, but with interest. That's why I stopped defending myself—time does the explaining better than I ever could."

The mist began to lift as the sun peeked through the clouds.

"To anyone wondering if they're enough—yes, you are. You're not replaceable. And when someone tries to trade your presence and ends up with emptiness? That's life teaching them their lesson, not yours."

He smiled at me, and it wasn't just comfort—it was legacy.

"These aren't just thoughts," he said. "They're anchors for when life feels unsteady. Hold onto them, and stay hopeful."

Those sacred mornings didn't give me answers wrapped in perfection. They gave me something better—clarity. Grandpa's voice became my compass, and every word he spoke lit a lantern in a place that had once been dark.

His final advice still echoes:

"Stay hopeful. Tomorrow hasn't arrived yet—and it might just surprise you."

XVIII

SELF-COMPASSION: NURTURING THE HEART WITHIN

Twilight had settled softly across the porch, and Grandpa's silhouette was framed by the fading glow of the sun. He didn't rush his words. He never did. Each one came like a lantern in the dark.

"Surround yourself with people who speak well of you even when you're not in the room," he began. "That's real friendship—when your name is safe even in your absence."

The breeze carried the scent of jasmine as he rocked gently beside me.

"Being raised right," he said, "has nothing to do with how you look or what you wear. It's how you treat others when no one's watching. That's where character lives."

He tilted his head toward the stars.

"The deepest lessons I ever learned came from empty hands and hungry days. Hardship strips away the noise and teaches you what truly matters."

Then, his voice firm:

"When someone shows you their true nature—believe them. Repeating the same hurt isn't an accident—it's a decision."

The swing creaked beneath us as he leaned forward.

"Fear? It only wins when you run from it. I used to fear so many things. Then they happened. And guess what? I'm still here."

He tapped the side of his chair.

"Your past was a classroom, not a sentence. Learn from it, then leave it behind. If you want to change your life, start by changing the way you think about yourself."

The stars grew brighter above us.

"And one last thing," he said, looking straight at me, "never be too busy for someone who's hurting. The silence you leave behind in those moments lasts longer than you think."

The night deepened, and with it, Grandpa's words grew softer, more inward—like they were meant to settle not just into my mind, but into my heart.

"Never let your emotions run ahead of your wisdom," he said quietly. "Stay calm, even when the storm tempts you to shout. A steady mind can save a breaking heart."

He gave a little nod.

"If even one person believes in you—really sees you—you're rich in a way most people aren't. Don't take that for granted."

I looked out into the darkness, remembering my own hesitations, the times I'd been afraid to act.

"That move you're scared of making?" he said, echoing my thoughts, "might be the one that changes your whole path. Don't wait too long to be brave."

He smiled at my silence, then added:

"Being a good person doesn't mean you'll keep everyone. It means you'll lose the ones who never deserved you. Let them go."

He chuckled lightly.

"Start saying 'no' when you need to. That's not selfish—it's survival. Boundaries aren't walls; they're fences around your peace."

Then, his tone softened into something more private.

"Solitude can be protection, not punishment. Being alone means no one can harm you—but don't forget, you're still someone worth caring for too."

We sat for a moment in the quiet.

"Everything," he said, eyes on the stars, "has a reason—even the ache. So don't think too far ahead. Just breathe. Sooner or later, it all makes sense."

I asked him, "Why do people only care when it's too late?"

He didn't speak right away—just nodded gently, his eyes holding the weight of a thousand moments.

Then, almost to himself, he said:

"Sometimes it's better to say nothing and smile. But don't lie to yourself. The real danger? It's knowing the truth, seeing the truth... and still clinging to the lie."

We both laughed softly at that—because it was harsh, and because it was true.

And as the stars shimmered above us, I knew that every moment I spent with Grandpa wasn't just conversation—it was a mirror. A map. A reminder that the way home is found not in perfect choices, but in honest reflection.

XIX

THE CURRENCY OF TRUST: A MORNING WITH GRANDPA

The morning sun filtered through the kitchen window, casting soft light across the table. Grandpa sat quietly with his coffee, his gaze calm and reflective—the kind of gaze that speaks volumes before any words are spoken.

"Time decides who you meet in life," he began gently. "But your heart decides who you want in your life, and your behavior decides who stays."

I nodded, already sensing the depth of the conversation to come.

"Trust," he said next, "is the most expensive thing in the world. It can take years to earn, and just seconds to lose."

He leaned forward slightly, tapping his cup.

"Don't let money change your attitude. It's meant for your pocket—not your personality. And it sure won't follow you to the grave."

I thought about how often people get lost in the pursuit of wealth, forgetting what truly matters.

"The biggest mistake I made," Grandpa admitted, "was letting people stay in my life far longer than they deserved. Sometimes it's hard to let go, but holding on can do more damage than leaving ever will."

I glanced down, thinking about my own relationships—the ones I'd held onto out of guilt, habit, or fear.

"You can always feel it," he added, as if reading my thoughts. "When someone's not being real with you, their energy speaks long before their words ever do. Energy never lies."

As we finished breakfast, his tone shifted.

"It's sad, you know—how many people stay in relationships, in jobs, in situations, just to keep things from falling apart. But in doing so, they fall apart themselves. They forget they matter too."

He tapped the table gently for emphasis.

"Peace doesn't live in money, or titles, or beauty. It lives in you—in the way you treat yourself when nobody else is watching."

We stepped out onto the porch again, settling into our usual spot on the swing. The breeze was soft, scented faintly with pine.

"No matter how good you are," he said, "someone will hate you for no reason. But don't let their bitterness stain your spirit. That's their storm to carry, not yours."

He paused, his gaze steady.

"People will gather allies—pretend to be the victim while carrying the poison. Don't get tangled in their story. Rise above it."

We rocked gently, the silence between his words growing fuller with meaning.

"Remember," he said, turning to me with a small smile, "shallow water makes the most noise. But deep waters? They stay still—and powerful."

As we sat there in the quiet, his words carved themselves into my heart.

"Don't be afraid to start over again. This time, you're not starting from scratch. You're starting from experience."

That same day, as the sun began its slow descent behind the trees, Grandpa offered more—words not planned, but flowing as naturally as the evening breeze.

"If she has a job, her own car, and lives comfortably," he said, watching the horizon, "understand this—she's not looking for money. She's looking for loyalty."

I smiled at his clarity. He always saw past appearances to what really mattered.

"You're lucky," he continued, "if you've got a sibling who's kind and selfless. Some only think about themselves—and they miss the whole point of having someone to walk through life with."

He paused, his expression turning thoughtful.

"People ask what you do for a living, not out of curiosity—but to decide how much respect to give you. It's sad. But it's true."

A soft breeze swept through the porch as if to carry the weight of his truth.

"But don't let their standards become your compass. It's not about what others think of you—it's about the quality of your actions. That's the measure of a person."

His words settled over me like a blanket of calm.

"You don't have to be strong every day," he said, voice softer now. "Sometimes you just need to be alone and let the tears come. That's not weakness—it's healing."

We sat quietly, listening to the crickets take over where the breeze left off.

"Do good for others," he said, "and good will come back to you. Maybe not today. Maybe not tomorrow. But it always finds its way home."

The porch darkened as the evening deepened, the stars just beginning to show themselves overhead.

And then, his final words for the day came, calm and unwavering:

"I never fake care. What I give—I give from the heart."

That day stayed with me—not because it was dramatic or loud, but because it was real. It was the day I realized that some of life's most powerful lessons arrive gently, dressed in ordinary moments, wrapped in silence, and rooted in truth.

And just like Grandpa said, deep waters stay quiet... but they carry the greatest strength.

XX

HOLDING IT TOGETHER: A GRANDFATHER'S STRUGGLE AND STRENGTH

He leaned against the table that morning with his usual calm smile—the kind that told you you were about to hear something real. His eyes, though warm, carried a weight, the kind built from a lifetime of holding it together when things tried to fall apart.

"They say narrow-minded people post vague things for attention," he began, chuckling, "but those who always take it personally—even when it's not about them—well, they're even narrower."

He paused, and the smile faded slightly. "I'm doing everything I can," he said softly, "to keep my life from falling into as many pieces as my heart already has."

Then came a truth wrapped in quiet admiration.

"When someone with more problems than you reaches out to help you—that's not just help. That's love. That's strength wrapped in grace."

He stirred his coffee, eyes thoughtful.

"Healing yourself? That might offend people who only liked you when you were broken. Some folks depended on your silence and your struggle."

After a beat, he grinned and tossed out one of his sharper truths.

"You're useless at home, but want to serve the barangay?" His humor always carried weight—this time, about misplaced ambition.

Then he got serious again, looking me straight in the eye. "Don't let anyone brainwash you into hating someone who never wronged you. Their issues aren't yours to carry."

We laughed together as he cracked another line.

"You're kind, but you're still a gossip. That makes you the Good Samare-tes." Beneath the joke, there was always a quiet nudge to be better.

He leaned back.

"Don't be too humble, and don't be too rude. Just treat people according to their attitude—it keeps things balanced."

His tone darkened slightly.

"People who backstab each other, then sit at the same table like nothing happened... they think loyalty is just convenience in disguise."

Then came the kind of wisdom only earned with time.

"The best revenge?" he said with a smile. "Just move on. Let karma handle the rest."

The breeze drifted in through the open door as he added, "Enjoy your youth. Because once you're married, trust me—you'll be folding laundry for the rest of your life."

His voice dropped lower, and he said seriously, "Don't fear the enemy who attacks you. Fear the fake friend who hugs you."

Then, smirking:

"Let's not pretend—everyone gossips a little. Just don't wear a halo while you're doing it."

And finally:

"Yes, I'm a nice person. But if you cross the line too many times, don't expect that version of me to stick around."

He stood up to leave, but then sat back down again, his expression shifting from playful to quietly burdened.

"I always hear, 'Will you ever run out of money?'" he muttered. "What do they think I am—the owner of SM?" He chuckled, but the fatigue in his voice was real.

Then, with a softer sigh, he added, "I don't need luxury. I just want peace. A simple life, without drama or debt—that's happiness."

Looking at me with quiet resolve, he said, "Avoid those who don't like you. They're not gold. You don't need to keep them."

His voice firmed again:

"They say life's too short to hold grudges. I say life's too short to let people keep disrespecting you."

Then he breathed deeply and softened.

"It's okay to get tired. It's okay to cry. Just don't quit. You can rest, but don't stop."

After a pause, he looked directly at me.

"My life. My choices. My mistakes. My lessons. Not yours to

judge."

And just when the weight of it all grew thick, he broke the silence with a grin.

"Buy your rice and groceries before spending on a hair rebond. Priorities, my dear. Hair can wait—hunger can't."

We laughed, but behind it was practical truth—his specialty.

Then he turned serious again.

"If you're rejected, accept it. If you're unloved, walk away. If they pick someone else, let them go. Every 'no' from someone is a 'yes' to your own worth."

His voice turned thoughtful.

"Don't fear the blunt ones—they'll tell you the truth to your face. Fear the sweet ones who stab you the moment you turn your back."

And then, raising an invisible glass, he laughed,
"Cheers to us who sing the wrong lyrics—but with full confidence."

He wiped a tear of laughter from his eye.

"Funny, isn't it? When you've got money, people treat you like honey. But when you're broke, you're more sour than kamias."

His gaze settled on mine.
"I am a limited edition. Once you lose me, you won't find another like me."

He grew quiet, then added:

"You know you're getting older when birthdays feel more like bills than celebrations."

And with a nostalgic smile:
"If you've kept the same mobile phone for five years—you're either loyal, stable, or too wise to waste money on what works just fine."

As night slowly crept in, he gave me his final words.

"No matter what kind of person you are—even if you have nothing in your pocket—you still deserve respect."

He stood then, walking away with the ease of someone who carried heavy things in silence and still made room to laugh.

And I sat there, his words still echoing—not just advice, but a reflection of resilience, boundaries, humor, and hard-earned truth.

He never tried to be perfect.

He just tried to be real.

And that was enough to change everything.

XXI

"INVESTING IN CONNECTIONS: THE VALUE OF RELATIONSHIPS"

He walked in that morning with the same steady presence as always—calm, measured, but carrying the kind of wisdom that speaks before the words even leave his mouth.

"If they don't involve you, don't get involved," he said simply, sipping his coffee. "If they don't tell you, don't ask. If they don't invite you, don't go. That's not pride—it's self-respect."

He paused and looked out the window, watching the breeze sway the trees in quiet rhythm. "Beauty," he added thoughtfully, "isn't about being thin or fat. It's about who you are when no one's looking—your heart, your character."

Then a grin broke across his face, teasing but sincere. "No matter how boring life gets," he chuckled, "never get married." He raised his eyebrows like a man who'd learned that lesson the long way around.

The smile faded slightly.

"You can't always stay silent and patient. Sometimes, you've got to speak up—so people don't get too comfortable underestimating you."

He leaned in a little, his voice sharpening.

"Never lie to someone who trusts you. And never trust someone who lies to you."

A sigh escaped him, as if he was releasing some old pain into the air.

"Forgive," he said quietly. "Even when there's no apology. Do it for yourself. A free heart is the one that learns to rest."

I nodded, absorbing the stillness in his tone.

"The worst moments in life?" he continued. "They show you the truth—the real colors of the people around you. And not everyone's palette is worth admiring."

He grew serious.

"If people hadn't been traumatized by cheating and betrayal, they wouldn't be so paranoid. We don't wake up with trust issues—they're taught to us."

He tapped his finger on the table.

"Don't waste time on people who don't respect, appreciate, or value you. You can't grow where you're not watered."

He looked me in the eyes.

"There's a difference between being frank and being rude. Frankness tells the truth—even when it stings. Rudeness just talks without thinking."

Then, in his grounded way, he offered one of his deepest truths:

"We aren't handed a good life or a bad one. We're just given a life. It's what we do with it that makes it one or the other."

He stood for a moment and said firmly, "Respect and camaraderie—those are two things money will never buy. If you've got those, you're already rich."

He turned solemn.

"It's not the lie that hurts," he said. "It's the part where I realize I can't trust you anymore. That's the wound that doesn't heal fast."

As he made his way to leave, he offered a final reminder.

"Don't feel bad if sometimes no one can help you. Everyone's carrying something heavy. Be kind—but don't forget yourself."

Later that day, the old man sat back down in his armchair, the light of the afternoon casting shadows across the floor. His voice still held the strength of morning, but with a deeper weight now.

"Haters?" he said with a smirk. "They only hate what they can't have—and who they can't be. Let 'em talk. That's their battle, not yours."

He tapped his chest lightly.
"That voice inside you—the one that speaks in quiet moments? That's your intuition. She knows. Trust her."

Then came one of his favorite sayings, one I'd heard many times but never tired of.

"If you're ever torn between being kind and being right," he said, "choose kind. That way, you're right where it matters most."

He leaned forward, his tone more serious.

"If someone wants to talk to you, they will. If they want to be in your life, they'll show up. Stop chasing after people who only offer you pieces when you're willing to give them your whole heart."

Then with a mischievous smile:

"I always said—move out, move on, move up, and move smarter. And don't rush it. Growth takes time."

His gaze darkened a little, firm and direct.

"Don't lie to me," he said. "I can handle mistakes. What I can't handle is dishonesty. That breaks something deeper."

He sat back again, quieter now.

"Worrying is like paying rent on a house you don't even live in. Let it go. Stay present."

He tapped his heart.

"Loyalty isn't taught. It's in you—or it's not. You'll know the difference when someone shows up for you without being asked."

A slow smile spread across his face.

"The day you stop caring what people think?" he said. "That's when you finally taste freedom. Most folks never get there—but you should."

He laughed gently, shaking his head.

"I've sat in rooms full of lies. And I smiled, because I already knew the truth. You learn to listen beyond words."

Then, with sudden weight, his voice lowered.

"A weak man? That's someone who lets others poison his loyalty—especially toward someone who's only ever stood by him."

His eyes drifted toward the window.

"People love blaming you until you step back. Then suddenly, their problems stay—and they realize they were never yours."

I asked him what success really meant, and he answered without hesitation.

"If you want to succeed, be ready to be doubted. Be ready to be tested. That's the only way to know if you really want it."

And finally, he gave the advice that settled over everything like a closing prayer.

"Stay away from people who can't admit when they're wrong, but never miss a chance to point out your flaws. That kind of energy will drown your peace."

His words weren't loud. They didn't need to be.

They were strong because they were true.

And the real gift wasn't just what he said—it was how he reminded me, without fail, to live right here... in the now.

XXII

THE COMPLEXITY OF LOVE: UNDERSTANDING HEARTS AND PAIN

The old father leaned back in his chair, the weight of the years resting in his shoulders but not in his voice. There was still fire there—still strength in the lessons he passed down with the quiet certainty of someone who had lived through every word he spoke.

"When you've got a good heart," he began, eyes focused out the window, "you help too much. You give too much. You love too deeply. And somehow," he said, voice softening, "you end up being the one who hurts the most."

He shook his head slowly, not in bitterness—but in understanding.

"I never cared to compete with others. Whatever I have, it's enough for me. Chasing after someone else's life only makes you lose your own."

He looked at me with quiet resolve.

"Sometimes your worst enemy is your own memory. It'll trap you in moments that no longer exist. Let it go when it starts knocking too loud."

He leaned in, serious now.

"Don't judge people who've loved more than once. You never know what they've survived to keep going. Love isn't always neat. Sometimes it's just brave."

His gaze didn't waver.

"The truth always finds its way out. So save yourself the trouble and live honestly. Lies might fix the moment, but they ruin everything after it."

Then came a sigh—one only parents know.

"Mothers," he said. "They nag, they scold, they repeat themselves a hundred times. But it's only because they care more than they show. And it hurts them deeply when their children stop listening."

He smiled faintly, as if hearing echoes of the past.

"I've seen kindness in people the world called ugly. And I've seen cruelty in faces that looked angelic. Don't ever let appearances be your compass."

He tapped the table once for emphasis.

"People will hate you without reason. Watch your every move—not because they care, but because they want something to gossip about. Let them. They don't know your truth."

His voice grew quieter.

"No one really notices your pain. Your sadness. But they'll catch every little mistake you make. That's the world—loud when you fall, quiet when you rise."

Then he said it plainly:

"Jealousy turns good people into shadows. They copy you, talk behind your back, and still want to be you. Don't let them disturb your peace."

He looked at me.

"Don't waste time explaining yourself to people who've already made up their mind. Talk all you want—they'll only hear what they want to."

He held my gaze.

"You've done more good than most people see. But the moment you mess up, they'll forget all of it. Still—keep doing good. Do it anyway."

He leaned back again.

"You don't owe everyone your story. Let your life do the talking. And let people believe what they want—it doesn't change the truth."

Then, with a sharp nod:

"People who act perfect—son, they're usually the ones hiding the most. Everyone's got a shadow. Best to check your own before pointing at someone else's."

He sighed again.

"People say life's too short to hold grudges. Maybe so. But it's definitely too short to keep letting people hurt you over and over. Set your boundaries. Enough is enough."

The sun dipped low, and he continued, quieter now, but just as certain.

"Before you try to show off," he said, "make sure what you're showing is real. Don't step on others to climb higher. It always costs more than it's worth."

Then he smiled, easing the tension.

"Stay strong. Life's gonna shake you. Just don't let it break you."

With a shrug and a grin:

"My life rule is simple—treat me well, and I'll treat you better. You get what you give."

He leaned forward, more serious now.

"Only trust the ones who see beyond your smile. The ones who understand why you fall silent, and where your anger really comes from. That's the kind of knowing you can't fake."

He looked out the window like he was watching a memory float by.

"You'll learn a lot about someone when they're drunk. That's when masks fall. Watch carefully."

Then, with a small laugh:

"I don't live for anyone else's approval. My life, my rules. If they don't like it, that's their problem."

A moment passed before he added:

"Blood doesn't always mean family. Sometimes, your true people are the ones who found you when you were lost—and stayed."

Then his voice grew firmer.

"If someone hates you, let them. They'll choke on their own bitterness. Hate always burns the one holding the match."

He looked at me with intent.

"Put your family first. If your wife and kids walk away, the friends you put before them won't be there to catch you. Learn that now—before it's too late."

He nodded as if sealing that truth.

"Being rich, educated, popular—it doesn't mean a damn thing if you're not kind. Be real. That's what lasts."

With a smirk:

"Don't be mad if your wife nags you about drinking. When you're sick in bed, she's the one holding the towel to your head. That's not control—it's love."

Then, tapping his temple lightly:

"Some days, I need a break from my own thoughts. It's heavy up here, son."

The room fell into a pause. He broke it gently:

"People respect money. That's just the world. But don't let their respect define your worth."

He smiled then, eyes warm.

"Surround yourself with those who bring out the best in you—not the stress in you. That's how you grow."

And as the light dimmed and the air settled, he said one final thing:

"A mother's scolding is loud, yes—but it's louder when it's gone. Be grateful for every word, even the harsh ones."

His words lingered like the scent of old pages—quiet, familiar, and unforgettable.

He didn't teach with lectures. He taught with truth.

And that truth stayed with me—long after he fell silent.

XXIII

STRENGTH, JUDGMENT, SELF-RESPECT, AND AUTHENTICITY

He sat upright, firm in posture, his voice steady with experience.

"My strength didn't come from lifting weights," he began. "It came from lifting myself up every time life knocked me down."

There was no bitterness in his tone—just truth.

"You don't know my story, my character, my heart," he said pointedly. "So don't judge me based on your assumptions."

He looked away for a moment, eyes distant.

"My doors are closed," he said quietly, "to those who left me when I needed them the most."

Then he shook his head, almost in disappointment.

"It's strange—some people are kind to strangers but cold to their own family. They find it easier to help outsiders than the people who raised or stood beside them."

Leaning forward, his eyes sharp, he added,

"When a toxic person can't control you anymore, they'll try to control how others see you. Let them twist the story. Truth doesn't panic—it waits."

With a smirk and a touch of warning:

"Before you speak, make sure your tongue is connected to your brain. There are a lot of educated people with terrible manners."

His voice softened.

"Don't let your feelings go too deep. People can change—sometimes overnight. And not always for the better."

Then, in his calm but clear way, he added,

"Get along with everyone. But don't trust everyone. A warm smile can hide a cold heart."

He sighed. "We're not all in the same boat, you know. We're in the same storm—but some have yachts, others have canoes, and some are drowning. So be kind. Always."

"Tell me," he asked, "have you noticed how people treat you based on how useful you are to them? When you're helpful, you're valued. When you're not? You're forgotten."

He lowered his voice.

"Trust is a dangerous game. Easy to give, hard to take back."

Then with a slow nod, he added,

"Don't ever be ashamed of who you are. Be real. That's what matters—not pretending, not showing off."

He smiled knowingly.

"If you think you're always right, you've learned nothing

from life."

His voice dipped into something deeper.

"You smile—but you know who the traitors are. You're kind—but you're no fool. And one day," he said with a laugh, "you'll reach an age where people's nonsense won't even bother you anymore. It's a beautiful thing."

The fire crackled softly as Grandpa leaned back again, his voice mellowed by the glow of the flames.

"You know, child," he began, "rich or poor doesn't matter much in the end. People chase after so much. But contentment—that's where real happiness lives."

He chuckled lightly, "It's not about who smiles in your face. It's about who defends your name when you're not there. That's loyalty."

He looked into the fire, reflective.

"Letting go... that's the hard part. They say hold on to the ones you love. But sometimes," he said slowly, "the strongest thing you can do is let them go."

Then, brightening, he grinned.

"You know Mr. Bean? Funny guy—but he taught me something: enjoy your own company. Don't wait around for someone to make you happy. You've got that power already."

He paused. "Sometimes tears come out of nowhere. And that's okay. Whether you fight or surrender—that choice is yours. But don't forget that pain passes, and so does the storm."

"Loyalty," he said next, "shouldn't be given to just anyone. Save it for the ones who never made you question theirs."

He leaned in.

"Even if you have nothing," he said softly, "you still deserve respect. That doesn't come from money. That comes from being human."

A smile tugged at the corner of his lips.
"And don't be too proud to apologize. You're wrong? Own it. Excuses just make the hole deeper."

Then came one of his favorites, said with a small chuckle:
"If they're jealous, if they argue, if they're emotional—it might just mean they care. Don't mistake fire for lack of love."

His expression grew more serious.
"If you believe that money makes you better than others, then you're actually the poorest soul of all. Riches aren't in your bank account. They're in your behavior."

"People who love you?" he said. "They don't run when things get messy. They stay. That's how you know it's real."

He looked at me, voice calm but resolute.

"Don't bother correcting fools—they'll hate you for it. Correct a wise person, and they'll thank you. That's how you tell who's worth your time."

He sank back into his chair.

"Patience, child. You can't rush what's meant to be. Some things take time—and that's not a delay. That's preparation."

Then came one of the deepest lessons.

"There comes a time when you have to stop crossing oceans for people who wouldn't even step over a puddle for you. Don't keep pouring into those who don't even notice when you're empty."

With a wry smile, he said,
"And remember—when you're quick to judge, you often mistake your own flaws as someone else's. Be careful. The mirror can be a painful teacher."

Grandpa's words weren't made for applause. They were made to live by. And like embers in a fire, they stayed warm long after they were spoken— reminding me who I was, and who I was still becoming.

XXIV

UNSEEN BATTLES, SILENT VICTORIES

Grandpa sat quietly, gazing into the fire, its light flickering in his tired eyes. After a long pause, he finally spoke.

"You know," he said gently, "if you've been hurt many times but still manage to smile, you're stronger than you think. The world throws all kinds of challenges your way, but true strength is found in those who keep going—silently, steadily."

He leaned back with a heavy sigh. "Losing someone you love," he continued, "that's one of the hardest pains to carry. But healing doesn't come all at once. It comes slowly, quietly. Let God take care of the wounds in your heart. Don't rush it—His timing is always perfect."

The firelight warmed his face as he looked over and said, "You can't go back and change how things started. That part's over. But you can still shape how it ends. And that's where your power lies."

A soft smile tugged at the corner of his mouth.

"Happiness," he said, "is a choice. That doesn't mean life will be easy. People will try to knock you down. But your joy? That's yours to protect. Don't let anyone steal it."

Then, more firmly: "And never, ever give up. The hardest battles are given to the strongest soldiers. That's you. You've got more fight in you than you know."

He shook his head and chuckled, "And when you chase your dreams, don't step on others to get there. You never know—the very person you step over today might've been the one who could've lifted you tomorrow."

A moment of silence followed before his expression turned somber.

"No matter how kind, loving, or loyal you are," he said softly, "some people will still walk away. And when they do, that's on them—not you."

He pointed toward the mantel, where a simple framed photo sat.

"Respect," he said, "isn't earned through diplomas or money. It's earned by how you treat people. I've known folks with barely any schooling, but more decency than men with fancy degrees."

Leaning in, his voice lowered.

"If someone can live peacefully without you, you can live peacefully without them too. Stop begging for space in places where you're not welcomed."

He straightened up, his tone resolute.

"Life ain't about how many problems you face—it's about how you face them. Stand tall. Don't let the storm decide who you are."

Then came a truth wrapped in a warning:

"Surround yourself with people who lift you. The ones who

push you forward—not drag you down. No room for drama or jealousy. That's dead weight."

He raised a finger for emphasis.

"When life gets too heavy, pray. Don't rant on Facebook. Don't wait for likes. Talk to the One who listens."

His eyes darkened for a moment.

"The most dangerous person in any room?" he asked. "Ain't the loudest. It's the one watching. Thinking. Quiet people see the most."

He shifted in his seat.

"Forgiveness," he said softly, "doesn't mean forgetting. Some wounds leave a mark, even after you've forgiven the person who made them."

The fire crackled as he leaned back.

"And don't you ever think beauty is just a face," he whispered. "It's in your heart, your dreams, your soul. That's what matters most."

The fire dimmed further, casting long shadows. Grandpa spoke again, his tone softer, but purposeful.

"Listen here," he said, "nobody's spotless. Everyone makes mistakes. But here's the good part—you can always turn around. You hear me? Redemption ain't earned by being perfect. It's earned by deciding to do better."

He paused, letting the words sink in.

"People will judge you," he said plainly. "That's just how the world works. But don't let it break you. They don't know your journey. They only see what they want to see."

A smile crossed his lips, the kind that comes with hard-earned wisdom.

"And don't be fooled," he added, "the ones who stand by you during the tough times? Those are your people. That's your tribe. Remember them."

His voice grew steady again.

"Real warriors ain't the ones who never fall. They're the ones who keep getting back up. Over and over again."

You nodded quietly. Every word rang true.

"Now listen," he said. "Sometimes, the best way to show your worth... is to pull back. Stop pouring your time and energy into people who take you for granted. When they notice you're gone, that's when they realize your value."

Then, with a final truth:

"Trust—it's the hardest thing to earn, and the easiest thing to lose. Once it's broken, it's never the same again. Guard it. Respect it. It's the foundation of every real relationship."

He leaned back once more, eyes resting on the last glowing embers in the hearth.

And in that quiet, where the fire faded and night fully took hold, his words remained—stronger than ever.

Not just a conversation.

Not just advice.

But a victory—a quiet, unseen one—shared from one warrior to another.

XXV

TRUE WEALTH: RISING ABOVE CRITICISM AND STAYING TRUE TO YOURSELF

Grandpa shifted in his chair, the fire casting a warm glow across his face as he looked around the room. His eyes gleamed with the kind of wisdom that only years of life could give. He took a deep breath and pointed to one of the quotes on the wall, a soft smile playing on his lips.

"You see that?" he said quietly. "It says to plant goodness if you want to reap goodness. Sounds simple, right? But the world forgets that. People are quick to judge, quick to take, and slow to give. But if you're always putting kindness into the world, you'll be surprised what comes back. It may not be instant, and it may not come from the people you expect—but life has a way of rewarding a good heart."

He chuckled, the sound warm and steady.

"As for being liked by everyone," he said, shaking his head, "don't lose sleep over it. Not everyone's gonna like you—and to be honest, not everyone's worth impressing. If you're happy with who you are, that's enough. Trying to please everyone? That's a recipe for misery."

His gaze drifted to another quote on the wall.

"Here's a truth for you: people will remember your mistakes more than your good deeds. No matter how much good you've done, they'll zoom in on your one bad day. But don't let that stop you. You're not defined by your worst moments. If someone can't see your efforts beyond your errors, let them go. That's their burden, not yours."

He paused, the fire reflecting off his thoughtful eyes.

"And about money..." he said slowly, "they say it's not everything—and they're right. But money does matter in this world. It opens doors. Still, it should never change who you are. Your real wealth is how you treat people. How you carry yourself. Integrity, kindness, self-respect—that's what lasts."

Grandpa leaned forward slightly.

"There will always be people who try to tear you down, who focus on your flaws. But you can't let that stop you. Motivate yourself. Keep pushing. You're stronger than you think—and no one can take that from you unless you let them."

He straightened up, voice firmer now.

"Nothing in this life is permanent. The highs, the lows—they pass. So don't get too comfortable in the good times, and don't lose hope in the hard ones. Life is movement. Stay grounded, and you'll weather it all."

The fire crackled again, warm and steady, as his tone softened.

"As you get older," he said, "you speak less and listen more. Life humbles you. You stop caring about the noise and start noticing the quiet truths. You realize most of the things you once stressed over don't matter."

He grinned. "Perfection? It's overrated. What matters is honesty—with yourself and with others. That's what counts. Not the image, not the mask—just the truth."

Then, raising his worn hands for a moment, he said, "Don't be ashamed of these," he smiled. "Wrinkled hands tell a story. They say you've worked hard. That you've endured. That you've shown up for others even when no one showed up for you."

His voice dropped to a gentle but strong tone. "Loyalty—it's either there or it's not. Don't chase after people who keep you guessing. Stay true to your values, even when others don't."

The flames danced on the walls as he continued, "Strong people—especially strong women—they don't whine. They handle things. Quietly, firmly. Without looking for pity. That's real strength."

He let the silence settle for a moment before adding, "My moral compass is simple: You treat me well, I'll treat you better. That's it. And if someone talks behind your back? Let them. That just means you're ahead of them."

He leaned in again, voice lower. "Letting go of people doesn't mean you never cared. Sometimes it just means you finally realized they weren't meant to stay. Appreciate the ones who do stay. They're rare."

With a sigh, he leaned back. "Life may not always give you what you want. You might not be rich in things, but if you're rich in peace, in laughter, in love—you're already ahead."

Then with a twinkle in his eye, he added, "Call me old-fashioned, but seeing others succeed makes me happy. I don't hold onto bitterness. There's too much joy to be found in this journey."

His voice turned tender. "In the end, it's about being honest with yourself. Be kind to those who deserve it, but don't waste your energy on those who take your kindness for granted."

He smiled once more, the glow of the fire warming the lines of his face. "Life doesn't have to be perfect. You don't need all the answers. Just live with purpose. Let everything else fall into place."

And as the fire crackled softly, Grandpa's words wrapped around the room like a blanket—comforting, steady, and true. Lessons passed not from books, but from a life well lived. Embers of insight, still glowing long after the fire burned low.

XXVI

UNSHAKABLE: LIVING WITH INTEGRITY AND SELF-RESPECT

Grandpa took a deep breath, his eyes reflecting the flickering light of the fire.

"You know," he began, voice steady, "sometimes in life, you'll come across people who just don't like you. Even when you've done nothing wrong. But here's the thing..." He leaned in slightly. "I'm 98% sure those people don't matter. Why? Because I don't care what they think."

His tone deepened with clarity.

"The ones who help you when you've got nothing—those are the people you hold close. They see your worth without needing to be impressed. Not the ones who try to drag you down just to feel taller."

He paused for a moment, watching the firelight dance. "It's not shameful to admit when you don't have much. What's shameful is being broke and still arrogant about it. Humility—that's what keeps you grounded, even when life tries to knock you off your feet."

Grandpa leaned back, his fingers brushing his chin. "You're going to have to swallow some hard pills in life. And one of the hardest? Realizing that some of the people you cared for... they didn't care for you at all. But you know what? That's okay. Because truth is better than pretending."

His voice took on a sharper edge. "You'll see people taking sides, backstabbing, acting like saints in public and snakes behind closed doors. But don't you get caught up in that. Stay true. A liar and a deceiver may hustle hard, but mark my words—they won't prosper in the end."

The room grew quiet, only the soft crackling of the fire remained.

"I passed through the hardest moments of my life alone," he said quietly. "And still, I kept going. While everyone thought I was okay, I was learning to stand on my own. That strength? It was always there. I just had to find it."

Then he looked you in the eye.

"Never lie to someone who trusts you. And never trust someone who lies to you. Integrity, my child—it's the one thing no one can take from you. You might enjoy the fruits of a lie today, but karma? She always shows up."

He gave a low chuckle, shaking his head.

"You might be kind, generous—even forgiving. But if someone crosses your line again and again, don't be afraid to draw that line in stone. Kindness isn't weakness. Sometimes, it's restraint."

His smile returned, eyes wrinkling at the corners.
"I've smiled at people who've whispered the worst about me, thinking it would shatter me. But here's the secret—they can't break you unless you let them."

Then, in his final words, he leaned forward and spoke with calm certainty:
"Life's too short to be weighed down by people who don't see your worth. Stay honest. Stay kind. And above all—stay true to who you are. Everything else will fall into place."

We shall continue in the next volume.

AFTERWORD

The legacy continues

As you reach the final pages of Grandpa's Inheritance, I invite you to pause and reflect—not just on the lessons within, but on your own story, your own roots, and the quiet wisdom you've received from those who came before you.

This book is more than a tribute to a grandfather's voice. It is a bridge between generations, a vessel of values, and a reminder that our elders carry treasures no gold could match—perspective, patience, resilience, and love.

These stories, though simple in tone, are deep in meaning. They remind us that life's greatest insights often come not from the loudest voices, but from the gentlest conversations, the humblest teachers, and the quiet strength found within our families.

May these words inspire you to cherish your heritage, hold fast to your dreams, and pass along your own truths with kindness and courage.

With gratitude,
Mr. Shaloom Niyomuvunyi

About The Author

Mr. Shaloom Niyomuvunyi, born in 1998, is an accomplished MBA graduate, creative writer, and passionate advocate for literature. He hails from the Kinigi sector of Musanze District in the Northern Province of Rwanda.

His journey with words began at a young age and blossomed into a powerful calling. What started as Ibiragano bya Sogokuru has now evolved into Grandpa's Inheritance—a heartfelt tribute to family wisdom, resilience, and generational truth.

Raised by his mother alongside his elder brother after the loss of his father in 1998, Shaloom's life is a story of perseverance. He traveled across borders to pursue his education, completing both his Bachelor's and Master's degrees in India—a testament to his unshakeable commitment to growth and learning.

Since 2019, Shaloom has been the CEO of Komera Business and Consulting Services Ltd, where he brings visionary leadership and a deep passion for uplifting others. Outside the boardroom, he finds joy in storytelling, music, and helping people pursue their dreams.

A firm believer in the power of faith and persistence, he lives by the words:

"Try and fail, but don't fail to try."

His life reflects the beauty of resilience and the strength of hope.

A Note To The Reader

Thank you for journeying through these pages.

If Grandpa's Inheritance spoke to you—if it reminded you of your own family, healed a quiet place in your heart, or gave you new strength—I would love to hear from you.

Feel free to connect, share your reflections, or follow updates on future works.

? Email: niyomuvunyis@gmail.com

? Socials: Instagram, Facebook, LinkedIn: shaloom Niyomuvunyi

Your support keeps these stories alive.

Coming Soon

Between Two Worlds: The Unspoken realities of the International Living.
The journey continues—with even more wisdom, humor, and heartfelt truth from the voices we need now more than ever.

Stay tuned.

FINAL BLESSING

May you live fully.
May you speak honestly.
May you honor your roots and raise others as you rise.
 And when you forget the way, may these pages help you find it again.

www.ingramcontent.com/pod-product-compliance
Lightning Source LLC
Chambersburg PA
CBHW021231130726
47988CB00002B/918